The
Snowball Effect

The
Snowball Effect

Deb Loughead

Orca currents

ORCA BOOK PUBLISHERS

Library and Archives Canada Cataloguing in Publication

Loughead, Deb, 1955-
The snowball effect / written by Deb Loughead.
(Orca currents)

Issued also in an electronic format.
ISBN 978-1-55469-371-9 (bound).--ISBN 978-1-55469-370-2 (pbk.)

I. Title. II. Series: Orca currents
PS8573.O8633S66 2010   JC813'.54   C2010-903586-0

First published in the United States, 2010
Library of Congress Control Number: 2010929084

Summary: After a snowballing prank causes a car accident,
Dylan deals with the guilt of lying about his involvement.

*Orca Book Publishers is dedicated to preserving the environment and has printed this
book on paper certified by the Forest Stewardship Council®.*

Orca Book Publishers gratefully acknowledges the support for its publishing
programs provided by the following agencies: the Government of Canada through
the Canada Book Fund and the Canada Council for the Arts, and the Province of
British Columbia through the BC Arts Council and
the Book Publishing Tax Credit.

Cover photography by Jupiter Images
Author photo by Steve Loughead

ORCA BOOK PUBLISHERS
PO Box 5626, Stn. B
Victoria, BC Canada
V8R 6S4

ORCA BOOK PUBLISHERS
PO Box 468
Custer, WA USA
98240-0468

www.orcabook.com
Printed and bound in Canada.

15 14 13 12 • 5 4 3 2

For Pat and Chip, Duncan and Sam

Chapter One

On Friday evening when Garrett called, I was in the mood for anything. I had my parka and my snow boots ready at the door. By six o'clock I was going antsy waiting for that call. I didn't want to spend the rest of the evening at home with my grandma. Gran was desperate for someone to play cards with her.

After three games of gin rummy, I needed to get out of the apartment.

"We're on at Matt's for tonight," Garrett told me. "You in?"

"Of course," I said. "The usual Friday-night feast. Wouldn't miss it!"

"Don't forget your balaclava," Garrett added. "For *after* the feast. You're sticking around for *that* too, right? You're not backing out on us, are ya, Dillweed?"

My stomach twisted, and I paused.

"Well?" Garrett said. "Can we count on you, or what?"

I hesitated for only a second. I didn't like to keep this guy waiting. "Yeah, sure. I guess I'm in. See ya in fifteen," I told him. Then I started hauling on my winter gear.

"If you're going out, can you pick me up a bag of Cheezies at the gas station?" Gran called from the kitchen, where she was playing a game of solitaire.

"Sure thing, Gran," I told her. "I'll grab some cash out of the sugar bowl."

Mom left some of her tip money for me and Gran to use whenever we needed it. She usually came home with some great tips from Rocky's Roadhouse, where she worked as a bartender. Wintertime brought in the best tips of all. The curlers dropped by on their way to the arena, or on their way home, and knocked back some pints. Hockey players stopped in too, after their games. In Bridgewood everything was within walking distance, and nobody worried about drinking and driving.

The exception was the snowmobilers. Those guys spent most of their free time riding snowmobiles on the trails that snaked through Bridgewood and cut a swath through the surrounding forests. They were decent guys, mostly, and Mom knew the law. She cut them off before they could be over the legal limit, and they respected her judgment.

"Make sure they're the good kind, not the no-name brand, okay?" my grandma called. "I can't stand those cheap, cheesy Cheezies. Ha!" She laughed out loud at her joke. "Get it, Dylan?"

"Yeah, I get it, Gran," I told her. "Hope you're not in a hurry though. I probably won't be home till eleven thirty or so."

"That's okay. I'll be waiting up for your mom anyway. There's a good movie starting at midnight, so I can just eat 'em then."

"See ya later, Gran," I called over my shoulder as I slammed out the door.

I ran all the way down the six flights of stairs instead of waiting for the elevator. When I burst through the front doors, I was punched in the nose by the windchill. My nostrils froze instantly. But the balaclava did a great job of protecting the rest of my face. The snow was crunchy underfoot. It was like walking on soda crackers. Winter had already set in with a vengeance, and it was only the beginning of December.

In this part of the country, Old Man Winter sinks his teeth in early and stays late. Usually by November he's settled in for the long haul. We get lake-effect snow, which happens when cold wind scoops moisture off the warmer lake water and dumps snow on us. A few inches of snow can fall in an hour. It's like living in a snow globe that someone's constantly shaking. Sure, it's pretty. Pretty annoying! But we're used to it around here. We find plenty to do for fun on a Friday night in the ice-cold darkness.

Overhead the stars were bright pinpoints in the sky, the moon barely a toenail clipping. For a change, there weren't any streamers of snow pouring off the lake tonight. I hurried along the sidewalk, sliding on patches of ice the way I always did. It was the closest I ever came to skating. Not having a dad to teach me or a mom who could afford the equipment, I'd never even learned to skate properly.

I knew how hard it was for Mom to scrape up cash for groceries and the bills, even with the help of Gran's pension. So I didn't complain much. Now that I was fifteen, it was embarrassing to go to the ice rink and have all my friends, guys *and* girls, zoom past while I hung on to the boards. I avoided that rink.

The closer I got to Matt's place, the louder my stomach grumbled. I could practically hear it talking to me through my jacket. Hanging out at Matt's was always the best part of Friday night. Matt's parents were really cool, especially his dad. He liked to play pool with us, or sometimes even poker. He loved cooking too, and he always made the four of us his sous-chefs.

When I got there, I walked right in without knocking on the back door. Their door was never locked. I tore off all my winter clothes and nearly sprinted to the kitchen. The guys were all gathered around the counter as usual. Garrett, Matt and Cory each had a task to do. Matt's mom was sitting at the table sipping a glass of wine while she watched the show.

"About time, Dillweed," Garrett said. "I planned on scarfing down all of yours if you didn't show up soon to help."

Matt and Cory laughed along with Garrett. I cringed, because I knew he probably meant it.

"Don't worry, I would have saved you some," Matt's dad said with a huge grin. He was a big guy with sandy hair and a wicked sense of humor. "I need you here on Friday nights. You're my chief cheese grater, you know. Wash your hands, buddy, 'cause it's pizza night and the oven's hot."

He handed me the block of cheese and the grater after I dried my hands. "Okay, get to work, Dylan," he said, then started rolling out pizza dough.

"How come Dylan always gets to grate?" Garrett said, struggling to chop the onions. "I hate doing onions. They always make my eyes water."

"Because Dylan's such a machine," Matt's dad told us. "Jeez, don't *cry* about it, Garrett," he added, then passed him a box of tissues.

We all snickered.

"Hah, that's just hilarious," Garrett said. He glowered at me, like he wished he was being called a machine instead of me. "My eyes are actually burning, you know."

"Oh, you'll survive," Matt's dad said, patting him on the back. "Suck it up, bub!"

"Yeah, you think chopping's hard. I get stuck pitting these olives," Matt complained. "It's impossible. Why don't we have the pitted ones this time?"

"And these disgusting anchovies totally reek." Cory grimaced as he tried to twist off the tin lid.

"Ever smelled Matt's hockey bag? Trust me, those anchovies are *roses*," Matt's dad said. "Boy, you guys are whining like little girls tonight. What's up with that?"

I laughed out loud.

"But, Dad, this is taking forever, and we're all starving," Matt said as he carefully pried out another olive pit.

"Well, don't drool all over the veggies and cheese, boys," his dad warned us. "Mom doesn't like extra sauce on her pizza."

"Okay, that's *gross*," Matt's mom said, rolling her eyes. "I guess I just don't get your goofy guy humor. And I think I just lost my appetite too."

"Great, my plan worked! More for us," Matt's dad said, and we all cracked up.

Chapter Two

By 8:00 the kitchen was all tidied, and Matt's parents were sitting by the fire. The four of us put on our winter gear and headed outside.

"We're just going over to the gas station to get some junk food for later," Matt yelled to his parents.

"Hurry back," Matt's dad called. "I'm gonna kick your butts at pool tonight."

A thrill fluttered in my chest as we charged through the snow-choked streets toward the bridge. When we took a shortcut through the gas station, I waved at Bud Wilkins, who was working the evening shift.

"Okay, you ready? Let's *do* this, dudes!" Garrett said, leading the way up the slippery incline to the top of the bridge. It was an overpass, and the main road through town ran right under it. It was the perfect spot for the Friday-night game of "snow-bombing."

That's what we called the ritual we'd started a few weeks back. It was Garrett's idea. We'd stand on the Forest Road bridge and watch the road below for approaching headlights. Then we'd bombard the passing cars with a volley of snowballs.

We'd laugh our guts out when the drivers honked and yelled curses at us out their windows. Sometimes the drivers circled around to try and find us on top of the bridge. But by the time they came back, we'd slithered back down the slope and disappeared into the wintry darkness.

It was a totally lame pastime, I'll be the first to admit. But when that's what your friends do for fun, either you go along with it, or you get called a wuss. I had lousy aim. I almost never managed to hit a windshield, and the other guys always laughed at me. But at least I was there, playing along with them, all for one and one for all.

We stood on the bridge, shivering in the howling wind. There weren't many travelers on the slippery road that night. In the distance we could hear the whine of sleds zipping along the trails that sliced across the frozen lake.

Then, finally, we saw the first set of headlights shining in the distance, heading northward into the night.

"Here we go, boys," Garrett yelled. He raised his arm to hurl the first frosty rocket. "Don't fire till you see the whites of their eyes!"

We had it perfectly timed. Firing just before the car reached the underpass was the best chance you had for smacking your target.

"Okay, fire away, guys!" Garrett yelled again. We all blasted our snow bombs over the railing.

"Yeah! Nailed it," Cory cried, raising his arms in triumph.

"Me too," Matt said.

"Me three!" Garrett told us.

"Missed again," I admitted after watching my snowball smash to bits on the road.

"Big surprise, Dylan," Garrett said. "Have you *ever* hit a car?"

"Hey, that guy didn't even honk at us." Matt sounded disappointed. "Maybe they just thought it was snow falling off the bridge or something."

"The snow's not wet enough," Garrett said. "The balls just fall apart on impact. We've got to give them something that they'll really notice."

He pulled a walnut-sized rock out of his pocket and held it up. "This should work just fine, boys. Here." Garrett handed us each our own rocks. "Try it. Come on. Hurry up, before we miss our chance. Hardly anyone's on the road tonight!"

He'd really come prepared tonight. It made me uneasy. Garrett always seemed to have a new surprise up his sleeve when he was looking for fun on Friday nights.

"Are you sure, Garrett?" I said, watching him squeeze the snow between his bare hands. The extra body heat always formed more solid balls, we'd discovered with practice. "That could break the windshield, don't ya think?"

"You wimpin' out on us again, Dillweed?" I hated it when Garrett called me that.

"I'm just sayin'," I told him as I stared at the rock in my hand.

"I dunno, Garrett," Cory said. "It's kinda dangerous, isn't it?"

"Oh, don't be such sucks, you guys. It's just gonna scare them, that's all," Matt told us. Cory and I stood there watching Garrett and Matt work their tightly packed balls of snow. We'd never used a rock inside a snowball before.

When I thought the others weren't watching, I dropped my rock over the bridge. When I looked over, Cory was staring at me. I just shrugged and grinned. Cory smirked, then dropped his own rock over the side. We both worked our snowballs into nice round comets, perfect for pitching.

Okay, so I *was* wimping out, but I really didn't want to do any damage.

And at least with Cory here, I had a fellow wimp. I wasn't the only one who thought the rock was a bad idea. Snow-bombing was a good time waster for a Friday night, but I didn't want to make trouble for anyone. I was a true wuss at heart, I guess.

"Okay, get ready," Garrett hollered. " 'Cause here comes one now!"

I watched the distant headlights approaching along the snow-covered road. It was so cold that even the salt-and-sand mix the town maintenance crews had spread could barely get a melt going. The car wasn't moving quickly. This cautious driver wasn't taking any chances on the slick roads tonight.

I felt a sudden pang of guilt at the thought of catching the person off guard and pummeling the car.

But when Garrett yelled "Fire," I fired.

And finally I did it! My snowball hit the roof of the car with a satisfying thump.

The other sound we heard, though, was the loud crack of a rock meeting a windshield. It wasn't a good sound.

The driver slammed on the brakes, and the car went into a spin and disappeared under the bridge. We heard metal scraping against concrete, followed by a sickening crunch and a tinkle of broken glass. Then nothing.

It's strange how deafening silence can be. The wind whipped little snow tornadoes around us as we stood there for a moment in disbelief.

Then we slowly leaned out over the guardrail for a better look. There was nothing to see below us except for skid marks in the snow.

"Crap," Cory said.

"Let's get out of here," Garrett said.

"I'm right behind you, dudes," Matt said.

"Are you all *crazy*?" I yelled at them. "We can't just run away and leave that car! What if somebody got hurt?"

"I'll call nine-one-one on my cell phone," Cory said. "The cops will be here in a second. But we can't stick around here. They'll know it was us!"

"I'm going down there," I told them, then spun around and headed for the slope.

"Don't do it," Garrett said. "You're the one who's nuts. You'll get caught, and then we'll all be screwed!"

"I'm going," I told them, then started sliding down on my butt.

My whole body had gone numb, and I couldn't even feel the cold anymore as I bumped and tumbled my way to the bottom. The voices of my friends and their thudding footsteps faded into the night as they bolted for cover.

Chapter Three

When I reached the bridge abutment, I was afraid to look. My feet felt frozen to the pavement, and a voice in my head was yelling, "Run for it while you still can, you moron!" But I didn't listen. I just couldn't leave that car there. I peered around the abutment and sucked in my breath at what I saw.

The car had crashed into the bridge wall. The front end on the driver's side was crumpled up like a crushed pop can. The headlights cast an eerie glow under there, and I could hear the car radio playing tinny music.

As I edged closer to the wreck, a panicky feeling surged inside of me. My blood was picking up speed in my veins as my heart hammered behind my ribs. I didn't have a clue what I should do next.

By then I was close enough to the car to see the driver slumped over the steering wheel. It was an old car, probably didn't even come equipped with air bags. The driver didn't seem to be moving at all. I had so hoped that the driver would be standing by the car and assessing the damage.

I had already made up a little lie about what I was doing there, to cover my butt. I was heading out to get some Cheezies for my grandmother, was what I'd say.

And when I heard the crash, I ran over to check on the driver. But no such luck. I didn't need my cover story. The driver wasn't moving at all.

There was an impact spot on the windshield where the rock had met its target. It was almost like a bullet hole, with a web of large and small cracks spreading out from the center. The side window was damaged too, as if the driver's head had smacked against the glass. I had a sick sinking feeling that I might be looking at a dead body, until I heard a low groan.

I shuffled over to the fogged window and pulled off my balaclava for a better look. Someone was stirring in there. The driver's head was moving. *Whew!* A pale face turned to look at me, a woman's face. She was wearing a thick tuque, pulled down low. There was blood trickling from her nostrils and a swollen, bloody welt on her cheek.

I could see her mouth moving, but a dorky Christmas song was playing in the car, so I couldn't hear what she was saying. I yanked on the door handle so I could try to help her somehow, then realized that it was stuck shut because of a deep dent.

I slipped and slithered around to the passenger door and hauled it open. The woman was still looking out the other window where I'd just been standing. I heard approaching sirens in the distance, and relief washed over me.

"Don't worry," I told her. "The para-medics are on the way. Everything will be fine soon, okay? Can I do anything to help you?"

She slowly twisted her head in my direction again. "My head is throbbing," she said. "Could you *please* turn off that bloody radio?"

In that instant I realized exactly who was behind the wheel of that car. I felt totally sick all over again.

I started blindly pushing buttons until I hit the right one.

"Thank god," she said in a strained voice. "What just happened, anyway?"

"I don't know," I told her. "I just got here. I heard a crash and came over to see what happened. And I found your car here." Sorta true.

"Wait a minute," she murmured. "I think something hit my car, just as I was driving under the bridge."

"Really?" I said. "I was just heading for the gas station to get some Cheezies for my grandma when I hear the crash. But I didn't see anything."

Was I trying too hard?

"I think I must have smashed my head," she told me. "I feel dazed. And my cheek hurts too." She touched the wound cautiously.

"It's bleeding. I'll get you some ice for it, okay?" I told her. I scrambled out of her car and grabbed one of the random chunks of ice by the side of the road. I wrapped it in a rag that I found on the floor and passed it to her. She dabbed it against her face.

"Ouch," she said. "I think that feels better, but I'm not sure yet. I'm freezing. Can you see a plaid blanket in the backseat?"

"Got it," I said. I reached over the front seat and grabbed it, then draped it carefully over her shivering shoulders.

"Thanks." She offered me a weak smile. "I'm afraid to move. I hope nothing's broken," she added.

The sirens were getting closer. I knew they'd have to be careful on the slippery roads, but I could already see the pulsating red and white flashes in the distance. It was a relief that she would be under the care of experts in a few seconds.

"The ambulance and police are almost here," I told her. "Look, I've gotta get going or my grandma will worry. She always worries herself sick if she hears sirens and I'm not home. I hope you'll be okay, ma'am."

"You're a sweet young man," she said. "You look familiar too. What's your name? Do you know my daughter, maybe? Her name is Monica."

"Um, no, I don't think so. Take care."

And I bolted, just like that. Took off under that bridge at warp speed and disappeared into the darkness just as the emergency vehicles skidded to a stop. When I looked back, paramedics were already swarming to her rescue.

It wasn't until a few minutes later that I realized I'd left my balaclava and gloves on the front seat of her car.

Chapter Four

I whipped my hood up over my head as I dashed through the dark toward the gas station. When I burst through the door into the fluorescent brightness of the Kwik Stop, a blast of warm air walloped my frozen face.

"Hey, little dude," Bud said as soon as he spotted me. "How's it goin'?

Freezin' out there tonight, huh? How's your mom, anyway?"

"Okay," I told him. "Working hard, as usual." I tried not to meet Bud's eyes and slipped into the snack aisle to get my stuff.

Bud Wilkins liked to blather on whenever anyone stopped by the gas station. He was bored like crazy working there, I figured. He always seemed desperate for someone to talk to. Right at that moment, though, with guilt probably shining like laser beams out of my eyes, I didn't want to stick around and yap with him.

"Hey, didn't you run past here a little while ago?" Bud asked. "You were wearing a balaclava though. I'd recognize that orange coat of yours anywhere." *Nuts!*

"Nope, wasn't me, Bud. I just got here. Didn't need my balaclava tonight. I just ran over here to pick up Cheezies for my grandmother," I said. "She had one of her crazy cravings. Must have been someone else you saw."

Now I was the one who was babbling. The last thing Bud needed was encouragement. I had to get out of there fast, or I'd be stuck talking to him for half an hour.

"Guess so." Bud frowned. "What's goin' on out there, anyways? Thought I heard a loud bang a while ago. And a bunch of emergency trucks just went flying past."

"I think there was an accident at the bridge or something. They all seemed to be stopping there." I rifled around in my pocket for change, still trying to avoid his eyes.

"Hey, you got a bit of blood on your hand," he said. "Did you cut yourself?"

"What?" I looked. There was blood on the side of my hand. My throat clenched. I could barely choke the next words out. "How did *that* happen?"

When I was handing her the rag with the chunk of ice wrapped in it. She must have had blood on her hand from the wound. And now her blood was on me!

"That's really weird," I stammered.

"Let's see," Bud said, reaching for my hand. "I think I've got a Band-Aid in my drawer. You can wash it off in the can and…"

"It's okay," I snapped and snatched my hand out of his reach. "I'm fine. Look, Bud, I'm in a hurry right now. See ya round."

I grabbed the bag of Cheezies off the counter and slammed out the door.

"Hey, you forgot your change," I heard him yell behind me. But there was no way I was going back in there!

The first thing I did when I was out of sight of the gas station was wash the blood off my hand. As I scrubbed at it with a clump of snow, I kept saying, "Out, damned spot." I think it was a quote from *Macbeth*. It was something my mom said whenever she tried to wash stains out of my clothes.

My hands were burning cold, but I didn't care—I could hardly feel it. I was so freaked out, I couldn't even think straight.

Do you know my daughter, maybe?

Yep, I knew her daughter. I knew her well. Monica Buckley was a girl in my class with shiny black hair, eyes the color of chocolate brownies, and dimples when she smiled.

And the four of us had made her mom crash her car with our stupid snow bombs.

I headed for home. I stayed on the side streets, avoiding the main road in case someone was looking for me. I churned through the snow ruts, wishing I'd just stayed home and played cards with Gran tonight. Right now a game of gin rummy at our wobbly kitchen table was the most comforting thought I could conjure.

I'd have even traded the last fifteen minutes for a few hours of Gran's corny jokes right about then.

Every house I passed had warm light spilling through the windows onto the snow. In some homes people were watching TV, in others they were sitting around the table having a late dinner. Everyone was safe inside their houses, where trouble wasn't chasing them.

Some houses had Christmas trees twinkling in their windows already. We hadn't put ours up yet. Mom didn't seem to have time for that these days, but she'd promised me and Gran that we'd buy one this Sunday. I wondered if I'd be in jail by Sunday.

I had to cross the main street again to get to our apartment. I was almost there. Only one more block to go.

I reached the driveway just as a police cruiser pulled up in front of our building. *Gulp.*

Chapter Five

I stopped in my tracks and didn't budge, hoping that they hadn't spotted me. Maybe I could sneak down the side of the building and use the back door. I spun around and started walking away. And a car horn honked. Crap!

"Hey, Dylan? Come over here a minute. I need to talk to you."

Sergeant Nicole Vance was one of the local police officers. She was also my mom's best friend from high school. Every kid in town knew her because she dropped by our school often. At least once a year she spoke at an assembly about boating and snowmobile safety. In a resort area, something nasty happens to somebody every single summer and winter.

I wasn't in a hurry to go over there and talk to her. I really felt like making a run for it, but that would have been a dead giveaway. So I scuffed my way across the snowy driveway to her car. She had the window down and was looking at me in her usual perceptive way. My face was burning with dread, and my whole body was shaking like there was an earthquake going on inside of me.

Her police dog, Prince, was in the back. His huge paws were hanging over the front seat, and he was stretching his neck to check out what was going on. Prince made me nervous. He was a shaggy German shepherd and looked totally terrifying. But Nicole had complete control over him. She called him the best partner an officer could ever hope to have.

"What's the matter?" she said. "You cold or something? You're not even wearing a hat or gloves. That's kinda crazy on a night like this, don't you think?"

"I just ran over to the Kwik Stop to get Cheezies for my grandma," I told her. I held up the bag like I was trying to prove something.

"Yeah, I know. I was just over there. Bud told me you had stopped in. That's why I showed up here. Thought you might have seen something."

Double crap!

That was when I noticed my balaclava and gloves on the car seat beside her.

Nicole was staring at me, her sharp blue eyes drilling a hole into my thoughts. She glanced over at my gear and then back at me.

"Know who these belong to?" she said.

"Yeah," I murmured, kicking at a chunk of ice with my heavy boot. I still couldn't meet her gaze. "They're mine."

"Dylan, Bud said that you had blood on your hand. I think I know what happened." I'd never seen Nicole look so serious, but I was sure a lot of bad guys had.

"Okay, so I left them there. In that lady's car," I admitted. "After I tried to help her. But I guess you figured that out already, didn't you?"

"Dylan, you did something *heroic* tonight!" said Nicole. "Why don't you want to take credit for it? That woman, Sarah Buckley, wants to know who you are. She wants to thank you. That's what she was telling everyone when she was getting loaded into the ambulance. She said you were wearing a puffy orange coat."

"So she's okay?" I murmured.

"I'm sure she'll be fine by tomorrow," Nicole told me. "She's just shaken up. How did you happen on that accident, anyway?"

"Um…I heard the crash when I was going to the gas station for Cheezies," I said. I stared at the ground so she wouldn't see the lie on my face. "So I ran over to see what happened. I didn't want to make a big deal of it, so I left when help showed up."

"But you ran past the gas station and waved at Bud before the crash even happened. He remembered your jacket. And he thought he saw some other kids too. It was a while after that when he heard a loud bang."

Triple Crap. "Um, no, that wasn't me. Like I said, I just went to the gas station for some snacks," I told her.

"That's odd. Bud is certain he saw you before all the emergency vehicles went by. And you came back after that. That's what he told me, anyway. Maybe he was mistaken." She shrugged.

God, I hated my jacket. Gran had found it for me at the Sally Ann. She said I should wear it to be more visible in the winter darkness and in the woods. She was always worried about something happening to me. And, boy, was I ever visible! Why had I been stupid enough to wear it for snow-bombing. Duh.

"Huh, that's really weird," I said. When I swallowed, I felt as if I had a walnut lodged in my throat. "And anyway, half the hunters in this town have coats this color."

"So did *you* call nine-one-one, Dylan?"

"Nope," I said, looking her in the eye. "I don't even own a cell phone." At least that wasn't a lie.

"Well, we're looking for a witness," Nicole said. "It looks like a rock or something hit the windshield. Did you happen to notice anything going on before the crash? Did you see anything, Dylan?"

"Nope, I didn't see anything, Nicole." I was chewing on my fingernails. Did that look guilty, or what?

"Don't be afraid to tell me if you know something." Nicole passed my gear through the window. "Think about it, okay? Maybe you'll remember something."

"Okay," I told her. "I'd better get inside now, or Gran will be worried. See ya round."

"Say hi to Stephanie and your grandma for me, Dylan. And take care of yourself, kiddo," she said as she closed her window.

"I will," I told her. "See ya, Nicole. And Prince!"

I ran inside as she drove off, tires crunching on the icy road. At the elevator I kept punching the button because it was taking so long. I was about to make a dash for the stairs when the doors finally opened. Slowest elevator on the planet!

Gran was standing in the entrance when I opened the door. She must have heard my key rattling in the lock.

"Where have you *been*?" she said, wrapping her arms around me and hugging hard. "I've been worried sick since I heard those sirens. And your friends keep calling and asking where you are. I was sure something happened!"

"Nothing happened, Gran." I handed her the Cheezies, kicked off my boots and shrugged out of my coat. "There was an accident at the bridge. Who's been calling, anyway?" And why, I wondered, were they calling me now?

"It was Garrett," Gran said. "He was looking for you. But I thought you were with them at Matt's place. I was really worried when he said you weren't there!"

"I was there, for pizza. But then I left Matt's to go out for snacks," I told her. "I went to check out the accident at the bridge when I saw all the flashing lights."

"You did?" Gran gasped. "Well, what happened?"

I knew that would get her attention! "A woman crashed her car. Guess she skidded in the snow and hit the wall. She's okay, though. After that I just went to the Kwik Stop and came home. I knew you'd be worried when you heard the sirens."

"You're such a sweet kid, Dylan," she said, ruffling my hair.

Yeah, real sweet, I thought. If only she knew the truth. I felt rotten to the core about the trail of lies I'd left behind me all evening. Like a snowball rolling downhill, my lie kept growing bigger and bigger. I wondered where it would stop.

When the phone rang a few minutes later, I grabbed it on the first ring.

"Dillweed," Garrett said when he heard my voice. I cringed. "Where are you? We've been waiting for you to show up back at Matt's place. We need to talk to you. What happened over there, anyway? Did you go look?"

"Yeah, I looked. She's okay. She's in the hospital. A cop told me."

I heard him suck in his breath. "You talked to a *cop*? When?"

"When she pulled up in front of my apartment. It was Sergeant Vance. She was waiting for me when I got home," I told him.

"So what did she want? What did you tell her?" There was a challenge in his voice.

"Nothing. I didn't tell her anything." I couldn't hide the anger in my voice. Garrett was more worried about himself than the driver of the car that had crashed *because* of us. Because of our lame booby-trapped snow bombs.

"Yeah, well, just keep your mouth shut about it, okay?" Garrett said before he hung up.

I put down the receiver, stared at the phone and tried to swallow the snowball-sized lump in my throat.

Chapter Six

I didn't sleep well that night. I tossed and turned until I heard my mom come home after 2:00 AM. My room was right beside the kitchen, so I could hear every word Mom and Gran said. Mom already knew all about the accident. And even worse, she'd already heard that I was at the scene, helping out the victim.

"The paramedics dropped by afterward. They were just finishing their shift," Mom was telling Gran. "When Sarah Buckley described the kid in the orange jacket who'd helped her, they knew right away that it was Dylan. Everybody in town knows that coat, I guess!"

That stupid, stupid coat!

"My stars! Why, he didn't even tell me that, Steph," Gran exclaimed. "I guess he's a reluctant hero. Maybe he's shy about the attention."

"I'll talk to him about it tomorrow," Mom said. "This might have shaken him up. For now, we'll let him sleep. He's had an exciting evening."

Little did she know how exciting. I punched my pillow and kicked at my blankets as if I was running a race. How could I face them in the morning? How could I face anyone with this guilt gnawing like a rat at my guts?

Should I just tell them the truth? If I did, though, Garrett, Cory and Matt might get arrested. Maybe even me too! We could wind up in juvenile court. It would be totally my fault. And Garrett would *never* let me forget it!

I buried myself under my covers to block out the sound of their voices. And I tried my best not to think about the snowball of lies that was rolling out of control.

On Saturday morning the ringing phone woke me up right in the middle of a dream. In the dream there were sirens and flashing lights, and I had blood all over my hands. I was running through deep, heavy snow and getting nowhere. Talk about a guilty conscience! I thought the phone was part of the dream, until Gran knocked hard on my door.

"Dylan! It's for you. It's a reporter from the paper. Quick. Come to the phone."

"Oh, crap!" Yes, I said it out loud.

"Dylan. *Language*!" Gran said. "Now hurry up. Get your butt moving."

I couldn't hurry. My whole body felt as if it was buried under an avalanche. I had to try and dig myself out.

"Tell them I'll call back," I told Gran. *In a couple of years*, I felt like adding.

The last thing I wanted to do was talk to a reporter.

"Don't be ridiculous. Get out here right now," Gran said. She gave my door another hard knuckle rap just to let me know she meant it.

"I've got a sore throat," I said from under my covers. "Leave me alone." I didn't feel like facing the day. I had to come up with an excuse. A sore throat seemed like a good one. Gran always worried that a sore throat was strep, and I'd die or something.

"What?" She opened my door a crack, peered in and frowned. "Just a sec, Dylan." Then she went back out to the kitchen. "Would you mind calling back later? Dylan is indisposed at the moment." Pause. "Okay, thanks. Bye now."

She came back with a thermometer in her hand.

"Let's see if you have a fever," she said.

"Mmmmow," I said, letting out a phony groan. Then I opened my mouth, and she popped the thermometer under my tongue. She stood there tapping her foot and humming a Christmas song, checking her watch every few seconds. When she took it out, she squinted as she tried to read the numbers.

"Where are your reading glasses, Gran?" I asked her. Mom and I were always asking her the same question. And Gran always gave the same answer.

"Not sure. I left them somewhere, I guess." She shrugged. "Careful where you're sitting till I find them, okay? I don't want to snap the arms off again. Can you read what it says there, Dylan?"

Perfect. "Maybe a little bit higher than normal," I fibbed. "It's hard to swallow." I gulped hard to show her what I meant. And it was actually true.

The latest fib was stuck in my throat with the rest of them.

I got to lie low for the rest of the day, faking my illness. Gran made me tea and toast and brought me the Saturday comics to read in bed. After lunch when Mom got up, she tried to talk to me about the accident. I just pointed at my throat and shook my head.

"Poor Dylan," she said, ruffling my hair and kissing my forehead. "He does a good deed and then winds up getting sick. Doesn't seem fair, does it? Hmm.

Your forehead doesn't feel hot. Maybe you're just shook up from last night."

"Maybe," I whispered in a hoarse voice.

"How about we get the Christmas tree tomorrow like I promised?" Mom said. "If you're feeling better. We can have a little tree-trimming celebration, with eggnog. There's something I need to talk to you about tomorrow at dinner-time too."

Mom's eyes strayed to my bedroom window, where fat lazy snowflakes were drifting to the ground. She sighed and closed her eyes like she was stuck in a dream. Then her lips curled into a mysterious smile.

I knew that smile. I'd seen it before. Whenever she met a new guy, she floated around smiling like that. I got a sinking feeling in the pit of my stomach. These things never turned out well for my mom, yet for some reason she kept trying. She was forever hunting for Prince Valiant and winding up with the Big Bad Wolf— not my idea of a good stepdad.

"Sounds good, Mom," I said in my best "sick" voice. I wriggled deeper under my covers and gave her a weak smile.

"Cool. After my shift tonight I'll bring you home something yummy for your lunch tomorrow, okay?" She patted my leg. "Some of those sweet potato fries that you like. And maybe if you're feeling better later this afternoon, you can go down to the storage room and haul out the Christmas boxes."

"Okay, Mom," I said. Then I pulled the covers over my head, wishing I could hibernate in my bed like a bear, safe and warm until spring.

Chapter Seven

I finally dragged myself out of bed around midafternoon. The reporter called twice more that day. I managed to avoid both calls. The first time I was in the shower, and the second time I was in the storage room digging out the Christmas boxes for Mom. Gran was thrilled that I was feeling better already. I let on that I still felt a bit lousy in case my "illness" had to get worse for some reason.

While Mom was at work, Gran and I spent the afternoon putting up decorations and lights in the windows. She loved Christmas and was really getting into the spirit. Ever since my Gramps passed away and Gran moved in, the three of us had become a team. Sure, it was annoying to live with two women sometimes. But I sucked it up, because where else was I supposed to live? And besides, Gran baked great bread, cakes and cookies!

Gran made us tortellini in cream sauce for dinner, and then we watched *National Lampoon's Christmas Vacation*. She laughed all the way through it, the way she does every year. And, as usual, she reminded me that it was Gramps's favorite Christmas flick too. But he used to cry during some parts, she added, and her eyes welled up with tears when she told me that. I wasn't sure she'd ever get over losing him.

Garrett called a couple of times that day too. I asked Gran to tell him I was sick and couldn't come to the phone. I didn't feel like talking to him, or to any of my friends. I wasn't sure how I'd feel about facing them at school on Monday either.

I figured my fake illness might come in handy next week if I still wanted to avoid facing the guys.

That night I zonked out on the sofa after the movie. Gran woke me at some point and steered me to bed. I didn't even hear Mom come home from work. The next time I opened my eyes, bright light was pouring in, and what looked like a solid sheet of snow was brushing up against the window. Another snow-globe day!

I reheated the sweet potato fries for breakfast and ate them dipped in mayo.

Mom and Gran never showed their faces that early, so nobody bugged me about my lousy breakfast. Then I sat in front of the TV and watched old cartoons all morning.

Just before noon Mom stumbled out in her tattered robe, rubbing her eyes.

"I'm so glad you're feeling better, Dylan," she said, pressing a palm against my forehead. "And that you got the Christmas stuff out. Excellent. We can go buy the tree as soon as I get my act together here."

She scratched her shoulder and shuffled into the bathroom. Poor Mom. It had to be a drag working in a bar, but she never complained. She said she liked talking to people, so what better job than being a bartender? But I knew that deep down she wished she could be something more, like maybe a social worker. That was her "someday dream," as she called it. She even read books about psychology in her rare spare time.

By the time we were ready to go pick out a tree, a few inches of new snow had already fallen. Mom, Gran and I bundled up and set out on foot for the Boy Scout Christmas tree lot. We planned to drag the tree back on an old wooden toboggan. I felt like a flashing neon sign walking around in that stupid orange jacket, but I didn't have anything else to wear. My other coat was way too small.

All the way to the lot I kept glancing over my shoulder in case someone was following me. Paranoid or what! I was afraid a police car would come screeching up beside us and I'd get cuffed and tossed in the backseat.

But only my friends and I knew the truth about Friday night. And they wouldn't be blabbing. I just wanted to avoid any more attention. I didn't want to talk about it anymore, to *anyone*!

With only a couple of weeks left until Christmas, the tree lot was busy with shoppers. It was hard choosing a tree, because so much snow had fallen that they were all buried and looked like a bunch of white mounds. The Boy Scout dads who were supervising sales were busy bouncing tree trunks on the ground to shake off the snow. Mom and Gran and I were trying to decide between a pine and a balsam fir tree when Nicole came walking up to us with her husband and little girl.

"Hey, you guys," she said, then gave my mom a quick hug. "I see we all have the same idea today. How about that kid of yours anyway, Steph? I'm sure you've heard all about it by now. Isn't he amazing?"

"Sure is," Mom said, wrapping an arm around my shoulders. "He never ceases to amaze me!"

Nicole was looking at me in a weird way. Or maybe it was just my imagination. It was as though she knew more than she was saying. I could feel myself sweating under my heavy clothes.

"We think we might know what caused the accident," she said, still watching me. "Kids pitching snowballs from the bridge. Probably had rocks in them."

Uh-oh, not good! I looked down and started crunching chunks of ice with the heel of my boot.

"No kidding?" Mom said. "Who would even think of doing such a lousy thing?" She stood there shaking her head. "So you got all your Christmas shopping done, Nic?"

"Almost," Nicole said.

"I'm freezing, Mom," I said. "Let's hurry up and pick out a tree."

I veered toward Gran and led her away while Mom and Nicole finished their little chat.

"The balsams have a nicer shape," Gran said. "There are more branches for ornaments. They're so pretty and old-fashioned-looking."

"But they're fifteen bucks more than the pine trees," Mom said as she sidled up to us. "I could buy a couple of nice roasts with that."

"I'll kick in the extra fifteen," Gran told her. "I don't mind. It's worth it. What do you think, Dylan?"

At that point, I wasn't thinking about anything other than how I might make a run for it without attracting attention, because someone with a huge camera was on the Boy Scout lot, taking photos of the families buying trees. And a smiling rosy-cheeked woman with a notepad was scribbling down the names of the people they were photographing. They were from the local paper, the *Bridgewood Weekly*.

I tried to hide behind some trees, behind my mom, behind a husky dad who was shaking snow off a pine.

But I was wearing that ridiculous jacket, and the photographer spotted me. I saw him nudge the other reporter, and suddenly they were both staring at me.

"It *is* you, isn't it?" the woman said as she approached me. "Everyone in town is talking about you!"

I looked over my shoulder as if I didn't know who she was talking to.

"Yeah, *you*," the guy with the camera said. "Dylan O'Connor, the local hero! We've been trying to get ahold of you. He snapped a couple of shots before I could duck out of the way.

"Can you tell us what happened on Friday night?" the woman said. "How you comforted the victim at the accident scene? This is such a great Christmas human-interest story." By then Mom and Gran were beside me with huge grins plastered across their faces. Behind them I spotted Nicole. Watching me?

"Dylan, this is your big moment," Mom said, pushing me toward the reporters. "Go for it. Tell them what happened on Friday night."

By then a crowd had gathered. Everyone was curious. Probably everyone in town had heard about the kid in the orange coat. Everyone wanted to hear about how I'd helped Sarah Buckley at the accident. Everyone wanted a piece of me.

And I didn't want any part of it!

Chapter Eight

By the time I'd finished babbling to the reporter, I really did feel sick. She told me that the story would be on the front page of the next edition of the *Bridgewood Weekly*. It was a small-town paper and came out only once a week. That meant I had until next Wednesday to worry myself even sicker about everyone's reactions to the story.

I kept it simple and managed to avoid any huge lies. I said I happened to be nearby when the accident occurred. True. I told them I felt I had to check and make sure the victim wasn't too badly hurt. True. I told them I didn't place the phone call. True. I told them that I was getting Cheezies at the station for Gran. True.

The whole time I was talking, the reporter was scribbling and the photographer was clicking his shutter. And everyone was watching. There were so many familiar faces in the crowd. I tried my best to avoid them all, especially Nicole's probing eyes. The photographer took one final shot of me, Mom and Gran with the tree we chose. By then the Boy Scout leaders insisted we have the tree for free because I was an example of a good Scout.

We thanked the scout leaders and loaded the tree onto the sled. As we walked away, everyone behind us was clapping. I felt like throwing up.

"I almost feel guilty for choosing the more expensive tree," Mom said as we were walking home. "We're cutting into the scouting profits. But really, I'm so proud of you, Dylan. You did a great job explaining things back there. I can't believe what you did on Friday night!"

I cringed when Mom put her arm around my shoulders and squeezed me. I didn't deserve that hug from her.

"Just think," Gran said. "If I hadn't had that craving for Cheezies, you might not have even been on the scene at all."

"If you say so, Ma," Mom said, laughing. "I guess *you're* a hero too."

But I *was* there, and I would have been there anyway, I felt like telling them, because of the stupid snow bombs. I had no clue why everyone was making such a big deal out of it either. I mean, it wasn't as if I'd saved her life.

But, like the reporter said, it was a good Christmas news story. And in a small town, they were hard to come by.

I only wished that I wasn't one of the main characters in the story.

While the chicken was roasting, we decorated the Christmas tree. It was just the right size. Gran kept stepping back to admire it as we added lights, shiny balls and tinsel. Mom was always sure to hang the goofy little felt and pinecone ornaments that I'd crafted at school from kindergarten to sixth grade. She was the proudest of those and hung each one in a place of honor, at the top near the star.

"Looks great," Mom said, sipping eggnog.

"Perfect," Gran said, sinking into an armchair and sighing.

We had turned off all the lights, and the tree was a rainbow blur against the window in our cramped little apartment. Outside, the snow was still falling in a thick, heavy curtain, backlit by the streetlights. It looked pretty festive in that room.

"So…," Mom said. I knew what was coming next. She probably felt better discussing it in a dark room so she wouldn't have to see the look on my face. "So I met this guy at the bar a couple of weeks ago." She paused.

"And…?" I said, tapping my foot.

"Be patient, Dylan," Gran said.

"*And*," Mom said, drawing the word out. She took a slurp of eggnog, as if she was stalling. "And I think I really like him," she blurted out.

I sighed. I couldn't help it.

"Do you have a problem with that, Dylan?" she said.

"I don't know," I said. "Is he a creep like the other ones?"

"Dylan!" Gran said.

"It's okay, Ma," my mom said. "He has a right to ask valid questions. It's not like my past choices were always good ones. But I think you both might approve of this guy. He has a great job with a law firm down in the city."

"Well, that sounds promising," Gran said.

"I *know*! Yay! He just came up here to sled with a friend a couple of weekends ago, and we hit it off. He came back this weekend to see me again. And he wants me to go down to the city to visit him some time." I heard her sigh. It was a happy sigh.

"So is he *married*?" I said.

"Dylan!" Gran reached over and swatted my knee. "Watch your talk!"

"Hope not," Mom said. "And that's a valid question too. But I trust this guy. He has honest eyes and a really sweet smile. He told me he's divorced, and I believe him."

"What's his name?" I asked.

"Brent," she told me. "Brent Sinclair. He's a real sweetie."

"Whatever you say, Mom," I said.

"He's coming again next weekend," Mom said. "I'd like you to meet him, Dylan. Next Friday evening at the bar. Okay? Will you do that for me? It's not like I need your approval or anything. But I really, *really* want you to like him!"

It was my turn to sigh again. "Okay, Mom. I'll show up," I told her.

"A toast to Christmas and new beginnings," Gran said with joy in her voice.

And we all clinked together our eggnog glasses in the tree-lit darkness.

While we were cleaning up after dinner, the phone rang and Gran grabbed it.

"It's for you, Dylan," Gran whispered. "It's a *girl*!"

"A girl?" I said, wide-eyed.

"Is this someone we should know about?" Mom asked, winking.

I rolled my eyes and took the phone from Gran. *A girl?*

"Hello?"

"Dylan? It's Monica." *Crap*.

"Oh, hi, Monica. What's up?" I said, playing dumb about her call.

"What's *up*?" She laughed. "As if you don't know! I heard about what you did for my mom on Friday night. I just wanted to thank you."

"You heard…you heard about it?" I said.

"Everyone in town has heard about it. But my friend was at the Christmas tree lot this afternoon, and she told me what happened. About the reporters and everything. And how people were clapping."

"It was no big deal, really," I said.

"But it *was*, Dylan. You checked on her, you gave her ice and put the blanket on her shoulders when she was shivering. My mom has a fractured cheekbone, you know. And her neck is really sore now, whiplash or something. But otherwise she's fine."

"I was glad to help, Monica. I really was. I couldn't just walk away from something like that. I had to check on her. Anyone would have done the same thing."

I thought of my three friends running away, and I winced.

"I wonder who those rats were, anyway, the ones who were throwing the snowballs. Sergeant Vance said they had rocks in them." Now she sounded close to tears. And I felt like puking.

"I dunno," I muttered. "Look, I'm just helping with the dinner dishes. I've gotta go now, Monica."

"Okay, and thanks again, Dylan. I can't wait to see you at school tomorrow. You and that bright orange coat of yours."

Her laugh was like bells. I guess she didn't hate the coat as much as I did!

"Yeah right, me and my neon coat," I said, stuttering out a laugh myself. "Bye."

When I hung up, Mom and Gran were staring at me.

"Why do you look like you just saw a ghost?" Mom said, frowning.

Oh, if she only knew.

Chapter Nine

On Monday morning when I climbed aboard the school bus, everyone clapped. Except for Cory, Matt and Garrett. They were sitting there stone-faced.

"Stop it, you guys," I told everyone on the bus. "It's no big deal."

I felt like a total fake. There was no way I deserved this much attention, but it didn't seem to be going away.

Monica had saved the seat beside her and patted it as I walked down the aisle to my usual spot beside Cory.

"Sit here, Dylan," she said.

"Are you sure, Monica?" I asked. Her best friend Callie always sat beside her on the bus, but today Callie was sitting one row back.

"Reserved for the hero," Callie told me as she patted the back of the seat. "Sit down right here, orange coat."

"Okay," I said, shrugging. *Stupid coat!*

"Hey, Dillweed," Garrett called from the back. "How come you're not sitting with us? Too good for us now that you're a hero?"

A few of the kids laughed nervously. Monica stood up and glowered at Garrett.

"Do you always have to be such a jerk?" she asked him.

I'd been wondering that myself for ages, but never had the guts to ask.

Garrett let out a bark of laughter, and then the driver told everyone to be quiet. The roads weren't great today after yesterday's snow dump, and the driver was taking his time on the winding highway.

"How's your mom today?" was all I could think of to say to Monica.

"Pretty good," Monica told me. "Way better today than she was on Saturday. She's actually planning to bake some Christmas cookies today for our skating party next Saturday. We have one every year. I was wondering…would you like to come, maybe? You can bring your mom and grandma too."

"Skating?" *Nuts!* "Um…my skates are too small," I told her.

"That's okay. You can borrow a pair from one of my brothers. We have all kinds of spares hanging around, since they're in hockey."

Nuts! "Well, we might have some sort of family function going on, but I'll check and let you know," I told her. *Family function?* How had I even come up with that? I was getting way too good at lying lately, which probably wasn't a good thing!

"Great," she said. Then the two of us sat beside each other in squirming silence the rest of the way to school.

My so-called heroics even made it to the morning announcements. Our principal, Mrs. Hardy, said how proud the staff and students were of what I had done. Then she asked the school for a round of applause. I could hear the clapping and cheering from all the classrooms as the din echoed through the hallways. I felt like hiding under my desk, but instead I sat there grinning sheepishly and staring at my clammy hands. My lie was so big now, it had a life of its own.

At lunch Cory cornered me in the washroom. And he didn't look calm, the way he and Matt and Garrett had looked on the bus. No, he looked absolutely sick, his face pale and his mouth a gloomy line. That was weird for a kid who was usually smiling.

"This is killing me, Dylan," he said. "I can't stand it. What we did was horrible."

"What about *me*?" I told him. "They're doing a feature about me in the paper on Wednesday. I'm a huge fake!"

"Yeah, I heard about it," Cory said. Of course he had. *Everyone* had! "That really sucks. But I feel guilty like crazy too."

"Whatever," I said. "At least you called nine-one-one. At least you're not a phony hero."

"Garrett says we can't let on that anything happened. That if we shut up about it, it will all blow over soon," he told me. "He says you're a knob for talking to the paper. And I'm supposed to tell you that if our names come up, you're doomed."

"Doomed? He *said* that? But I didn't go to the paper! They came to me," I said, a little too loudly.

"Well, he doesn't believe that," Cory said. "He thinks you love all the attention."

"Tell him I hate it," I said as I dried off my hands and headed for the door. "And tell him that I'm not feeling so good about him lately either. No, leave that part out."

"Neither am I," Cory admitted as he trailed behind me along the hallway. "Want to hang out Friday night? They're playing pool at Matt's again, but I don't feel like it."

"I have to go to Rocky's and meet someone that night," I told him. "Why don't you come with me? I don't really feel like going over to Matt's place either."

I didn't mention that those Friday nights at Matt's hanging out with his cool dad would be hard for me to give up.

"Sounds good," Cory said. "God, I wish we hadn't done that. But at least we didn't have rocks in *our* snowballs."

"That doesn't make it much better, does it?" I told him. "Because we were still there, and we were *still* doing it, and we've done it before too."

"Well, I'm never doing it again," Cory said.

"Me neither," I said. Then we high-fived each other and headed for the cafeteria.

By the time school let out that day, I'd had enough. All my teachers had given me pats on the back, and I got bright smiles from everyone in the hallways. Somehow I'd managed to avoid coming face-to-face with Garrett. But every time he looked my way, I could read the expression on his face: *Keep your mouth shut, Dillweed.* I was starting to get a sore throat too. It felt as if my fake illness was turning into a real one.

When the school bus rolled into town around 4:00, I had made up my mind. I asked the driver to let me off midtown.

I headed straight for the *Bridgewood Weekly* office, a little hole-in-the-wall storefront on the main drag.

Both the photographer and the reporter were sitting at shabby desks staring at their computers when I walked in.

"Hey, Dylan," the photographer said. "How's it going? Got any more heroics to report?"

"I'd like to speak to the editor," I told them.

"You're looking at her," the reporter told me. "We both wear a few hats around here." Then she frowned. "You look upset. Why don't you sit down?"

I sat on a hard plastic chair and stared at them. I didn't even know where to begin. I cleared my throat and tapped my fingers on the desk.

"So it's like this," I said, then started to explain.

As I talked, their faces morphed into expressions of disbelief and surprise. But they didn't interrupt. They just let me babble.

I didn't even tell them the true version of the story. I left a lot out, especially the part about who was involved with the snow-bombing, because who knew what Garrett would do if I ratted him out?

So I said I was the only one there. I told them I snow-bombed cars for kicks on Friday nights. I said that after the car crashed, guilt got the best of me, and I went to check on the driver before running off into the night. My story wound down, and then I sat in silence staring at the floor.

"Really? You actually *caused* the accident in the first place?" the photographer said. "Hmm. The plot thickens." He looked over at the reporter and raised his eyebrows.

"*And*," I added, "I don't want you to print the story. It's not fair to Sarah Buckley, or to all the people in town. I feel like a big fake."

"Maybe so," the reporter said. "But you know something, Dylan? This is the story now. We can't *not* print it!" She shrugged and smiled at me. "Thanks for being so honest. Terrific tale, bud!"

That was the absolute last thing I wanted to hear.

Chapter Ten

As I stumbled along the snowy streets on the way home from the newspaper office, my sore throat got worse. What had started out as a scratchy feeling was quickly turning into a knife-sharp pain that made me wince when I swallowed.

It looked as if I really *was* getting sick. Maybe I was just sick of the crazy stuff that was going on in my life.

I couldn't believe that the *Bridgewood Weekly* was planning to print the story anyway.

Gran was knitting in her favorite chair, watching the Weather Channel, when I got home. The tree and the window lights were on, and she was basking in the rainbow glow. But she frowned as soon as she saw my face.

"What's wrong?" she said. "Something happened today. I can tell."

"It's nothing, Gran," I said as I hung up my coat. "I just have a sore throat, that's all. I think I'll go lie down till dinner."

"Come over and let me feel your forehead," Gran said.

"What's with you and Mom and your forehead fixations?" I asked in a thick gravelly voice. But I submitted to her cool palm. Her eyes grew wide.

"You're burning up," she said. "Go to bed right now. I'll bring you Tylenol and a glass of juice. I made chicken noodle soup for dinner. Talk about good timing."

It felt great to lie down. By then I had chills, all my joints were starting to ache and my head was throbbing. Gran brought me the Tylenol and juice, and a steaming mug of soup. I could barely swallow the gel cap. There was no way I could handle that soup.

I'm pretty sure I fell asleep in seconds. A while later I heard two voices, and my eyes fluttered open. In the smudgy darkness Mom and Gran hovered over my bed, looking down at me. Gran took away the soup, and Mom sat on my bed and put her hand on my forehead.

"Gran called me at work and I came home early," she said. "I'm taking you to the health clinic in the morning, okay? I'm borrowing a car so we don't have to walk. You're a mess, Dylan. I'm worried."

I couldn't answer her, couldn't even keep my eyes open. I fell asleep with her cool hand on my scorching forehead.

The doctor at the clinic said it was strep throat. Mine was the third case he'd seen that morning, he told us. He said it seemed to be going around the school. He prescribed some antibiotics and recommended that I stay home from school for the next day or two. That was the best news I'd heard in ages.

"You won't be contagious after about twenty-four hours on these meds," he explained. "But you won't feel one hundred percent for a while. Probably be feeling great by the weekend though."

"Gee, Dylan, don't look so sad about missing school," Mom said when she saw my smile. "Oh well, I guess they don't do much the week before

Christmas break. You don't even have classes on Friday, huh?"

I shook my head and smiled even wider. This was going to work out just fine.

For the rest of Tuesday I was buried under blankets on the sofa. I read and played cards with Gran and watched the odd TV show. Gran waited on me, bringing tea and soup and ginger ale whenever I needed it. It was almost like a "stay of execution," that peaceful day at home before the newspaper came out. Wednesday was doomsday, as far as I was concerned. By the end of the day the whole town would know what a jerk I really was.

Wednesday after lunch my sore throat was nearly gone, but I still felt achy and tired. I hoped I'd feel lousy for the rest of the week so I wouldn't have to face anyone until the New Year. Maybe by then the whole thing would have blown over.

The first phone call came late in the afternoon. Luckily Mom was at work. Midweek she worked the noon until eight shift, so she wasn't there to see Gran's eyes bug out of her head while she listened to the voice on the other end of the line.

Gran's face went slack as she hung up the phone. I knew what was happening. Gran was the first person to be disappointed with me today—the first of many.

"I'm going down to the lobby to get a copy of today's paper," she said. Then she hurried out of the apartment. I burrowed under the blankets on the sofa and waited.

I was still buried under there when she came back up. And I stayed under those blankets while she sat down, turned on a lamp and read the article. I was peeking out, trying to gauge her feelings by watching her face. I was so nervous I could feel my heart pounding in my throat.

"So, Dylan," she finally said. "What on earth were you and Cory *thinking*? How could you do something as ridiculously dangerous as that? Pitching snowballs with rocks in them? Honestly, I thought you were smarter than that. This is so disappointing."

"I know, Gran," I said. Then I kicked off the blankets and sat upright. *Huh?*

"What do you mean *Cory*? What about Cory? Why is *he* mentioned in the article? I didn't say anything about him."

"Well, it says here that you both contacted the newspaper office to tell your stories. Cory said he was on the scene too. He told them you were the real hero for going to check on the victim, and that he was a coward for running away. He does say he called nine-one-one though. I can't believe you were both up on that bridge in the first place. Why?"

"Wow," I said. "He told them. He actually went to the newspaper office and told them."

Gran wasn't hearing me. She was still studying the article and shaking her head. "I wonder what your mom will have to say about this, Dylan. She's going to be so disappointed. Honestly, what were you *thinking*?"

My whole body was starting to quake. It was the way Gran was staring at me with disapproval in her eyes. And maybe even a bit of sadness. I couldn't handle it.

"I guess I *wasn't* thinking, Gran," I told her, my voice strained. "It was dumb, okay? I admit it. Don't you think I feel guilty enough already? Don't you think I know how mad Mom will be? Crap."

"Dylan! *Language*!" Gran said.

"Oh, just leave me alone, will you!" I said.

I jumped up and stomped down the hall to my bedroom, then slammed the door so hard behind me that the windows rattled. Poor Gran. She had no idea why I was being such a jerk to her. But I just couldn't help it.

All that guilt was making me feel like a lit firecracker—any second I might explode!

Chapter Eleven

I didn't even turn the light on in my room. I just flopped down on my bed and lay in the twilight. I watched the reflection of headlights on the ceiling as cars drove past the apartment on the street below.

What *was* I thinking? A valid question, as Mom liked to say. And the only answer I could come up with was something that nobody would ever understand. And it was something that I was too embarrassed to actually admit.

I did it so I could hang out with Matt's dad on Friday nights. Garrett and Matt were best friends. That was why I put up with Garrett and all his stupid ideas. How lame was *that*? But I couldn't resist, because it felt as though Matt's dad was my surrogate dad. He treated us all like one of his own kids.

I loved the relationship Matt had with his dad. They were so close, and I totally envied that. I could never admit that to my mom and grandmother. Mom had a hard enough time as it was. The last thing she needed was a guilt trip from me, the poor kid who was deprived of a dad.

Gran left me alone. The phone kept ringing, and I could hear her talking in a low distressed tone. She kept telling people that she didn't know what had gotten into me, and that I was "a good kid deep down." What was *that* supposed to mean? I hated how I'd gone from hero to zero overnight.

That great rolling snowball of a lie had broken to bits at the bottom of the hill.

Gran didn't talk to me all through our omelet dinner. Her face was twisted in thought. She chewed slowly and stared into space. She glanced at me now and again and shook her head. It was making me crazy.

"Well, *say* something," I finally said. "Don't just sit there staring at me. I know you have a million questions."

"You told me not to talk to you, Dylan," she said into her plate.

I sighed and rolled my eyes. "Okay, I'm sorry," I said. "What do you want to know?"

"Why you did it," she said.

"I can't even explain that to myself," I told her. I pushed a hunk of green pepper around the plate with my fork.

It was hard to meet her eyes. "It's just something I did. So I could be one of the guys, I guess."

"Bad choice, Dylan," she said, shaking her head.

"Do you think I don't *know* that?" I said, slamming down my fork.

When the phone rang a second later, I launched myself across the room to answer, just so I could get away from Gran.

"Dylan, we saw the newspaper, and I need to tell you something." It was Monica's voice, flat and dull. Not good.

"Go ahead," I told her. By then I was ready for anything.

"You'd better not come to our party Saturday night. I don't think my mom wants to see you." And then she said it too. "We were so disappointed when we read what really happened that night."

"It's okay," I said. "I totally understand, Monica. And tell her I'm

really sorry for letting everyone down."
I hung up the phone before she could say
another word.

When Mom walked through the door
at eight, I could tell by the stressed look
on her face that she knew.

"It's snowing again," she said, kicking
off her boots. "Like we need more snow."

"Stephanie, did you see the…?" Gran
said, shaking the newspaper at Mom.

"Yeah, I saw it," Mom said. "And
I've talked about it with everyone who
walked into the bar today. I'm sick of
talking about it. I think I'll take a long
hot bath. I'm exhausted."

As she walked down the hallway,
I looked over at Gran and shrugged.

"This isn't over yet, Dylan," Gran said.

As if I didn't know *that*.

I avoided my mom by going to bed
before she finished her bath. And I stayed
in bed on Thursday until she left for work.
I didn't bother going to school that day

either. It was the last day of class before the holidays, so it didn't really matter.

Cory called after school to find out why I'd been away since Tuesday. I told him about my strep throat, then started asking a few questions.

"So why did you do it?" I said. "Why did you go to the paper, anyway?"

"You read the article, didn't you?" Cory said. "I couldn't take it anymore. I told you how lousy I felt. I called the paper to tell them my side of the story the evening after we talked."

"Right after I was in there," I said. "I guess I should thank you for doing that. But I'm in deep crap now. Everyone's mad at me here."

"Me too," Cory said. "I'm totally grounded. I won't be able to go out with you on Friday night. Nice photo of you and your mom and grandma in the paper, by the way. I heard you got your Christmas tree for free."

"Yeah, for setting a good example that I didn't even set," I told him. "Maybe I should pay the Scouts back for that tree."

"Maybe you should. Go for it, Dylan," Cory said before he hung up.

Should I? The more I thought about it, the better it sounded. I needed to make amends for what I'd done. I needed to prove that I wasn't the complete jerk that that everyone thought I was.

I had a bit of money saved up from doing odd jobs. Sometimes after a big snowfall I wandered through the streets with my shovel, asking people if they wanted me to dig out their driveways and walkways. And during the past summer I'd helped out at the marina. True, I'd spent a lot of my cash on video games and junk food, but I'd managed to save a bit.

When I counted it up, there was eighty-five bucks stuffed in a sock in my drawer. I had planned to buy Christmas gifts with that money—an extra pair of reading glasses and some new sock yarn for Gran and a book and some bath stuff for Mom. I crammed the money into my wallet, headed for the door and started yanking on my winter gear.

"Where do you think *you're* going," Gran said, glancing up from her knitting.

"Out for a while," I told her. "I'll be back in time for dinner."

I slammed out the door before she could try to stop me.

Chapter Twelve

It was another snow-globe night. Snowflakes were falling thick and fast and sticking to everything. The temperature had risen a few degrees since last weekend's deep freeze. This was perfect snowball-making snow. I actually shuddered just thinking about it.

My first stop was the Boy Scout Christmas tree lot. With just over a week until Christmas, their tree supply was pretty low. Two Scout dads were standing around laughing and talking and stomping their feet to keep warm. When they saw me coming, though, they stopped talking and stared.

"I can't believe he'd show up here," one of them said loud enough that I could hear.

"Maybe he's looking for another free tree," the other one said, and then they both snickered. I felt like turning around and running, but I didn't.

"No, I'm here to pay for the one you gave us," I said. Then I dug my wallet out and handed over fifty bucks. "Keep the change. Put it toward the Scouts," I added before I spun around and walked away.

"Thanks," they both said in surprised voices. But I didn't look back.

My next stop was the drugstore. I went straight to the snack and candy aisle looking for the right gift. There were boxes of chocolates and truffles decorated with Christmas wrap, but I picked out something else. It was a snack mix in a wheel-shaped tray, with nuts, chocolate raisins and gumdrops. It was tied up with curly red and green ribbon. I bought it and headed back out into the snow.

I knew exactly where Monica lived, one street up from the lake. I'd passed her house often in the summer on my way to the marina. I tramped along through the snow, but slowed down as I got closer. *Should I?* Maybe this was a huge mistake. What if they slammed the door in my face?

I stopped under a streetlight, trying to decide what to do next. I gazed upward at the dizzy spinning flakes. They stuck to my eyelashes and soaked my face, and gave me the crazy sensation that I was falling backward in space. I brushed them away with my sleeve, took a deep breath and headed straight for Monica's place.

Their tidy gray house was all lit up for Christmas, with a wreath on the door, a tree in the front window and electric candles in the other windows. It looked amazing, all warm and glowing on the snowy night. I dragged my feet up the walkway to the front door. Then I knocked.

Monica's mother answered. Her cheek was still bruised from the accident, and the cut had scabbed over. Her face fell when she saw me.

"Oh, it's you," she said.

"Yeah, it's me," I said. "I think we need to talk."

Mrs. Buckley frowned. "You sure about this?" she said.

I nodded, and she held the door open. "Well, come on in then, but stomp that snow off your feet first." I stomped and stepped inside, and came face-to-face with Monica, who was standing in the hallway.

She didn't look thrilled. "What are you *doing*?" she said. "I asked you not to come here." She sidled up to her mom and slipped a protective arm around her waist.

"It's okay, hon," Mrs. Buckley said, patting Monica's arm. "I invited Dylan inside. He wants to talk."

I stepped out of my boots, but didn't take my coat off. Then I stood in the hallway, holding the bag out and feeling totally awkward.

"What's this?" Mrs. Buckley said as she took it from me.

"It's a peace offering," I told her. "It comes with an apology and an explanation. But only if you're interested in hearing it."

"I think we'd better sit down," she said and led me into the living room.

Monica and her mom sat on the sofa. I couldn't even look at them. I sat on the edge of an armchair, my hands in tight fists on my lap. I stared at my knees.

Under that lousy orange jacket, I was sweating like mad.

"Relax, Dylan," Mrs. Buckley said. "So what did you want to tell me?"

And then I started talking. I explained what had happened that night, how scared I was when her car crashed. I told them how sorry I was for the trouble I'd caused, how sorry I was that they had to find out the truth from that article in the newspaper. Then I ran out of words and stared at my hands.

There was silence in that room for a few moments. I felt totally sick inside.

"I can't believe you did this," Monica's mom finally said.

"I can't believe I did it either," I said, practically choking on the words. But when I looked up, expecting fury on her face, I realized that she was smiling.

"No, I mean *this*, Dylan. Coming here tonight with a gift to apologize to me. It was just such a sweet thing to do."

"It *was*?" I said.

"Yeah, it was," she said. "And I really appreciate it. Look, the boys and their dad are at hockey tonight. I've got a big pot of chili on the stove for later. Why don't you stay for dinner and we can talk some more?"

"Really?" I said.

"Really," she said, grinning. Then she opened the bag and pulled out the gift. "Mmm. This looks yummy. I can use it for the party on Saturday night. You're coming, aren't you? With your mom and grandma? Monica told me she invited you."

"Um…," I said. "I'm not sure." I looked over at Monica. She was staring at me with a strange look in her chocolate-brownie eyes. Then she stood up and walked straight out of the room.

"Monica?" her mom said.

I was on my feet in an instant. "Maybe I'd better go," I told her, then made a beeline for the front door.

Before I could haul my boots on and make a run for it though, Monica was back, holding out a pair of skates.

"Why don't you try these on, see if they fit, Dylan," she said. "Maybe you can wear them Saturday night."

"Set them down by the door, Monica," Mrs. Buckley said. "He can take them when he leaves. You'd better call home though, Dylan. Let them know you're staying for dinner."

I blinked. I grinned. I took my jacket off.

Chapter Thirteen

When I walked out of Monica's house a couple of hours later with her brother's skates, I felt totally awesome. I felt like running through the streets yelling about how happy I was. I was ready to talk to my mom now. I figured I was ready for anything.

On the way through town I stopped off at Stedman's to do my Christmas shopping. I found a discount yarn bin and chose some thick blue stuff that Gran could probably knit into a scarf. What did I know about yarn anyway? I didn't have enough to buy reading glasses too, so we'd all have to watch where we were sitting. Then I found a discount book bin and picked out a couple of novels with interesting covers for my mom. She'd have to wait until Mother's Day for her bath oil. I left the store with less than two bucks in my pocket. Time to start saving again.

The one thing I wasn't ready for that evening was meeting Garrett and Matt. And that's exactly what happened when I was nearly home. They came charging out of a side street, laughing their faces off, and practically knocked me over.

"Dillweed!" Garrett said. "What's going on? Want to come and shoot some pool over at Matt's? Because, this week, Thursday night's the new Friday night. No school tomorrow! Yee-haw!"

"Nope," I told them. "I've got to get home. I was just out doing some shopping." I held up my bag to show them.

"Whatever," Garrett said. "Come on. Let's get moving, Matt! Didn't you say your dad's making pizzas tonight?" He churned through the snow and left me standing there beside Matt.

"You sure you don't want to come?" Matt said as he started walking backward.

He had no clue how badly I wanted to go.

"No thanks, Matt," I said.

Matt shrugged and turned and walked away. I had to force myself not to follow him. Then he stopped again and looked back at me. "Hey, I meant to thank you for not ratting on me and Garrett. I'd probably get grounded for life if my dad found out."

This time I shrugged.

"Okay, see ya." Matt crossed the road and disappeared into the snowy darkness, and I headed for home.

Before I could take even a couple of steps, I heard the sound of a dog barking not far off. Then I saw it coming along the street Matt and Garrett had just come charging from themselves. Someone had it on a leash, and it was pulling like crazy and barking its shaggy, scary head off.

When they stopped under a streetlight, I realized that Sergeant Nicole Vance was on the other end of the leash. The next thing I knew, Prince was leading her right up to my feet.

"Nice night for a walk," I said when they reached me.

"Dylan?" Nicole looked shocked. "Are you kidding me? It wasn't you *again*, was it?"

"What are you talking about? What wasn't me?" I said, frowning.

"Whoever rolled a huge snowball out into the middle of the road for Bud Wilkins to hit with his pickup truck about ten minutes ago," she said. She stared me down with suspicion in her eyes. "He's okay, but this crap has got to stop. Why did Prince lead me straight to you, Dylan?"

I sighed. "Because I was just talking to *them*, Nicole," I said. I pointed in the direction that Matt and Garrett had taken a minute ago.

"Thanks," she said. "I owe you one, Dylan."

Prince had picked up the scent again and was straining at his leash to cross the road. "They were there last Friday night too, weren't they?" Nicole asked. "I figured someone else had been with you and Cory. But you were afraid to tell me, right?"

I just looked at her and shrugged.

"So Prince is a tracking dog too?" I asked her.

"He's trained for everything," she said. She flicked me a wave and took off with the dog. I couldn't even imagine what would happen when Nicole and Prince showed up at Matt's door in a few minutes and busted them. His dad was going to be so disappointed in him. And I knew exactly what *that* felt like.

Gran watched me the whole time I was taking off my coat and boots. She pretended to be knitting, but I saw her looking over the top of her glasses. I knew she was dying to find out about my dinner at the Buckleys' place.

"Hey, Gran," I said.

"Hi, Dylan! Did you have a good time tonight?" She smiled brightly, waiting for my answer.

"Sure did," I told her. I left the skates by the door, then zipped into my room to hide my presents under the bed before she could begin the interrogation.

I decided to stay in my room. I relaxed on my bed listening to my favorite punk CD. I wanted to wait till Mom got home before I started talking. Since it was a Thursday night and after eight o'clock, that would be soon.

When I heard the door slam a little while later, I sat up on the side of my bed. Then I sucked in a deep breath and headed for the living room. Mom was already stretched out on the sofa after a long day of standing behind the bar. She looked over at me and blinked slowly, and I knew it was time.

"Mom, Gran, there's some stuff we need to talk about," I said.

"Darn right, Dylan," Mom said, sitting up and patting the seat beside her. "Nicole dropped into the bar just as I was leaving. And she told me a very interesting story."

Before I had a chance to even open my mouth, Mom started telling Gran about everything that had happened over the past week. Mom knew all the details, because Matt had blabbed everything the instant Nicole and Prince showed up at his front door.

Gran sat there with her knitting needles in midair, gaping at Mom, then me, and then back at Mom again. "Well, now I've heard everything," she said, shaking her head.

"Not everything yet," Mom said. "I also heard that Dylan went to the Boy Scout lot and paid for that Christmas tree today."

No secrets in this town, *ever*!

"He did? Isn't that something," Gran said, reaching out and ruffling my hair. "Like I've been telling everyone, Dylan, deep down you really *are* a good kid."

"Guess I made a major mistake in judgment," I admitted.

"We all do that sometimes, Dylan," Mom said. She wrapped her arms around me and squeezed.

"Okay, so you already know everything," I said, squeezing her back. "But did you know that we're all invited to a party at Monica's place Saturday night?"

"Nope," Mom said. "But I heard you had dinner there tonight."

"What? Who told you that? Are there spies in this town, or what?"

Mom nudged me and laughed. "Gran called me at the bar after you phoned her. Bet you had a nice time there. Sarah Buckley is great. She and her husband have dinner at Rocky's sometimes. So what's this about a party, anyway?"

"It's a skating and caroling party," I told them. "Monica even loaned me a pair of her brother's hockey skates." Thinking about how stupid I'd look on the ice made me cringe.

"I'm not sure I can skate anymore," Gran said, looking worried. "But I'm pretty sure I can still sing okay. I think I'll bake some icebox cookies for the party."

"Those are my faves! That would be great, Gran." Then I looked over at Mom. "Do you think you can get off work that night, Mom? So we can all go?"

"I've already booked it off," Mom said, looking mysterious. "I'm supposed to go out with Brent that night, you know. We kind of have a date."

"You do? Okay, so do you think maybe he'd like to come along too?" I couldn't believe I was even saying that.

"Wow! How can you say that when you haven't even met him yet, Dylan?" Mom asked, wide-eyed.

"Because I trust your judgment, Mom."

"Well, guess what?" Mom grinned. "Brent can't skate. In fact, I was going to take him over to the rink Saturday night to help him learn. I'll probably have to hold him up the whole time."

Perfect!

"Know what, Mom?" I told her. "I think I'm starting to like this guy already."

Deb Loughead is the author of numerous books for children and young adults. She has written extensively for the educational market, and is the co-editor of *Cleavage: Breakaway Fiction for Real Girls* (Sumach Press, 2008). This is Deb's second novel for the Currents series. She lives in Toronto, Ontario.

Titles in the Series

orca currents